DATE DUE

planet EARTH

Earth's Crust and Core

By Amy Bauman

Science curriculum consultant: Suzy Gazlay, M.A.,
science curriculum resource teacher

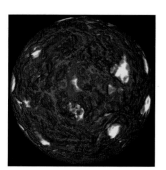

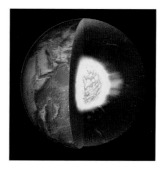

Gareth Stevens
Publishing

Please visit our web site at www.garethstevens.com.
For a free catalog describing our list of high-quality books, call 1-800-542-2595 (USA)
or 1-800-387-3178 (Canada). Our fax: 1-877-542-2596

Library of Congress Cataloging-in-Publication Data available upon request from the publisher.

ISBN-13: 978-0-8368-8915-4 (lib. bdg.)
ISBN-10: 0-8368-8915-0 (lib. bdg.)
ISBN-13: 978-0-8368-8922-2 (softcover)
ISBN-10: 0-8368-8922-3 (softcover)

This North American edition first published in 2008 by
Gareth Stevens Publishing
A Weekly Reader® Company
1 Reader's Digest Road
Pleasantville, NY 10570-7000 USA

This U.S. edition copyright © 2008 by Gareth Stevens, Inc. Original edition copyright © 2007 by ticktock Media Ltd.
First published in Great Britain in 2007 by ticktock Media Ltd., Unit 2, Orchard Business Centre, North Farm Road,
Tunbridge Wells, Kent, TN2 3XF United Kingdom

ticktock project editor: Ruth Owen
ticktock picture researcher: Ruth Owen
ticktock project designer: Emma Randall
With thanks to: Suzy Gazlay, Terry Jennings, Jean Coppendale, and Elizabeth Wiggans

Gareth Stevens Editor: Brian Fitzgerald
Gareth Stevens Creative Director: Lisa Donovan
Gareth Stevens Graphic Designer: Keith Plechaty

Picture credits (t = top; b = bottom; c = center; l = left; r = right):
Corbis: 23bl. iStockphoto: 15cr. NASA: 4l, 4ct, 4cc, 4b, 4–5 main, 7br, 29tr. National Oceanic and Atmospheric
Administration: 21br. Natural History Museum: 16bl. NHPA: 19l. Photolibrary Group: cover. PlanetObserver –
www.planetobserver.com: 16–17 main. Reuters: 23tl. Shutterstock: 1 all, 3, 5tr, 5cr, 5br, 6tl, 7tr, 7cr, 8–9 main, 9c, 9tr, 9cr,
9br, 10tl, 10cl, 10–11 main, 11tr, 11cr, 13tr, 13bl, 14tl, 14b, 14–15c, 17tr, 19tr, 20tl, 20–21 main, 21tr, 24–25 main, 24br,
26tl, 26bl, 27bl, 29cr, 30–31 all. Science Photo Library: 16tl, 16cl, 22b, 28tl, 28cl, 28–29 main. Superstock: 6–7 main, 6bl,
12–13 main, 21tcr, 25tr. ticktock Media Ltd: 4cb, 8tl, 8bl, 10bl, 18t, 18bl, 19cr, 19br, 20bl, 22l, 23r, 24l, 25br, 27tl, 29br.

Every effort has been made to trace copyright holders, and we apologize in advance for any omissions. We would be pleased
to insert the appropriate acknowledgments in any subsequent edition of this publication.

Printed in the United States of America

1 2 3 4 5 6 7 8 9 10 09 08 07

CONTENTS

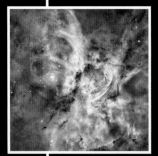

The Moon is 221,000 miles (355,670 kilometers) from Earth when the two are closest.

From a cloud of gas and dust...

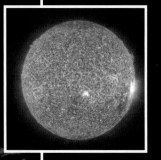

...our Sun was born. Rocks, metal, and dust were left over from the Sun's birth. They became...

...the planets of our solar system, including Earth.

CHAPTER 1:
Our Amazing Planet

We may not feel it, but Earth is always moving. Earth circles the Sun at about 67,000 miles (108,000 kilometers) per hour. Earth is mostly made of rock. Yet from distant space, it looks blue. That is because Earth's surface has vast areas of water. The large green areas are plant life springing from the land. Move closer, and you can see its amazing mountains and valleys.

BIRTH OF THE PLANET

Earth is part of a **solar system**. It is one of eight planets that **orbit**, or circle, the Sun. Our planet's history began more than 4.5 billion years ago. At that time, the solar system was only a cloud of dust and gas. The huge cloud floated in space. Then dust and gas inside the cloud caved in.

Out of the dust and gas came a new star—our Sun. Dust that was left over went spinning around the Sun. The dust started to stick together, forming rocks. Some of these rocks were small enough to fit in your hand. Others were as large as mountains. Many of these rocks joined together in space. Over time, they built up into planets. One of these planets was Earth.

Earth is about 93 million miles (150 million km) from the Sun. As the third planet from the Sun, its position is "just right." It is neither too hot nor too cold. The temperature makes life possible.

PLANET EARTH FACTS

EARTH'S INGREDIENTS
Most of Earth is made up of eight major **elements**. Elements are substances that are made up of just one type of atom. The elements silicon and oxygen make up about 75 percent of Earth's rocks.

THE BLUE MARBLE
Earth is one-of-a-kind in the solar system. Its surface is covered with water in liquid form. Without this water, there would be no life on planet Earth.

AN EARTH YEAR
It takes Earth just over 365 days (one year) to orbit the Sun. How much longer? Add another six hours, nine minutes, and 10 seconds, to be more exact.

BIRTH OF THE MOON
The Moon is Earth's only natural **satellite**. A satellite is any body that circles another body in space. Our Moon probably formed after Earth did. It is likely that a huge space rock hit Earth. That collision created debris. Debris is the remains of something that has been destroyed. Over time, the debris came together in space to form the Moon.

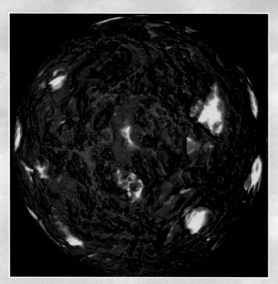

This art shows Earth as it may have looked billions of years ago. As Earth was forming, so were the seven other planets in our solar system. About 4.3 billion years ago, our solar system took shape.

EARTH'S EARLY YEARS

When Earth was young, it was pounded by debris from space. The planet's surface heated and melted. Scientists believe Earth was a huge sea of hot rock and metal. Each new bit of **matter** added to the mix. Bit by bit, the planet grew.

The melted rock sent nitrogen, carbon dioxide, and **water vapor** into the air. The stream of space debris added dust. At this time, the **atmosphere** formed. It was probably dark, dusty, and poisonous at first!

Over time, a **crust** formed on Earth's surface. Experts are not sure when this happened. But rocks about 3.8 billion years old have been found in Canada. By that time, the surface must have been growing solid.

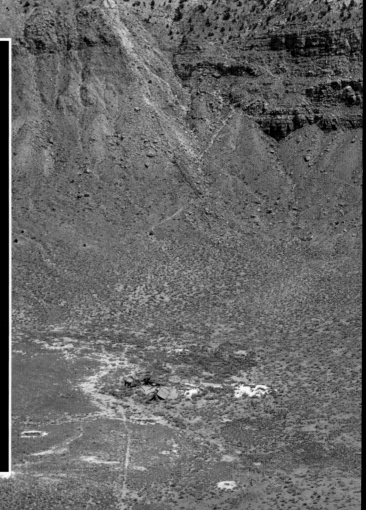

DISAPPEARING DINOS

Impact craters are holes on Earth's surface that are caused by rocks from space. The craters form when space rocks, such as meteorites and **asteroids**, hit. The Chicxulub Crater in Mexico is a huge impact crater. It is 106 miles (170 km) wide. The asteroid or meteorite that formed it must have been gigantic. The event probably caused **earthquakes**, firestorms, and more. Some scientists believe this event even caused the dinosaurs to disappear. This crater formed about 65 million years ago.

METEORITES

Today, bits of rock and metal still shoot through space. Most of them burn up when they hit Earth's atmosphere. But sometimes they make it to the surface. When they do, we call them meteorites.

PROOF OF PAST IMPACTS

Scientists say that over the past billion years there have been thousands of hits. The hits are called impacts. About 130,000 impacts have produced craters that are at least a half mile (0.8 km) wide.

The Meteor Crater is in Arizona. It formed between 20,000 and 50,000 years ago. The crater measures 0.7 miles (1.2 km) wide. It was made by an asteroid. It was the first crater to be labeled an impact crater.

SPACE JUNK

The debris in the solar system is often one of these three forms:

METEORS/METEORITES

Meteors are chunks of rock and metal. As they enter Earth's atmosphere, they burn. They make streaks of light called shooting stars. A meteor that hits Earth is known as a meteorite.

ASTEROIDS

Asteroids are bigger space rocks that orbit the Sun. Most are found between Mars and Jupiter. That area is called the asteroid belt. Some asteroids are nearly 670 miles (1,000 km) across.

COMETS

Comets are balls of frozen gas, dust, and rock. As a comet gets close to the Sun, some of the ice melts. This releases dust, which forms a tail. Comet tails can be millions of miles or kilometers long.

PLANET EARTH: INSIDE AND OUT

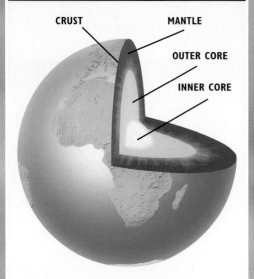

CRUST   MANTLE

OUTER CORE

INNER CORE

DIAMETER AT THE EQUATOR:
7,926 miles (12,756 km)

DIAMETER AT THE POLES:
7,900 miles (12,714 km)

DISTANCE FROM THE SUN:
93,000,000 miles (150,000,000 km)

AVERAGE SURFACE TEMPERATURE:
59° Fahrenheit (15° Celsius)

THE PLANET AS WE KNOW IT

Earth's surface cooled and formed a crust. But the planet stayed hot inside. Melted rock, called **magma**, flowed inside Earth. Sometimes, the magma burst out onto the surface of the planet.

These events sent water up into the atmosphere. Comets dropped more water down from space. The air took the water in. Water gathered in the air and then rained back down.

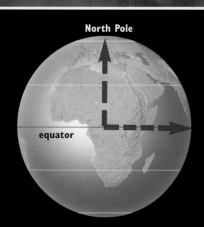

North Pole

equator

MEASURING INSIDE OUT

Earth is not a perfect sphere. You can tell by measuring its **radius** at different places. Radius is the distance from the center of a sphere or circle to the outside. The distance from Earth's center to its poles is a certain distance. The distance from the center to the equator is about 26 miles (42 km) wider. This shows that Earth is not a perfect sphere.

The water filled low spots on Earth's surface. Oceans, lakes, and rivers formed. Earth, as we know it, began to take shape.

The layers of Earth fell into place. As the planet cooled, it divided into three layers. We call the three layers the crust, the **mantle**, and the **core**.

Mount Chimborazo is located in Ecuador, a country in South America. It is the highest mountain that sits on the equator. The diameter of Earth is greater at the equator than at the poles. Therefore, the top of this mountain is the farthest point from Earth's center!

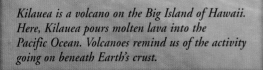

Kilauea is a volcano on the Big Island of Hawaii. Here, Kilauea pours molten lava into the Pacific Ocean. Volcanoes remind us of the activity going on beneath Earth's crust.

MELTING EARTH

SHAPING FROM WITHIN

Here, magma is seen beneath Earth's crust. **Lava** is magma that has reached the surface. When lava pours from beneath the crust, it shapes the surface. This is one way that land formed on our planet.

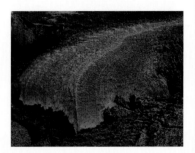

ADDING TO THE LAND

New lava flows out and over past lava flows. The lava cools and hardens at uneven speeds.

NEW GROUND

Lava and ash from **volcanoes** cool and form hillsides. Water, wind, heat, and cold break down the rocks. Wind and water carry sand and debris to other places. Soil forms, and seeds in the soil grow into plants.

HIGHS AND LOWS

MOUNT EVEREST
Mount Everest is in the Himalayas, a mountain range in Asia. Everest is the highest point on Earth. It stands 29,035 feet (8,850 meters) tall.

THE DEAD SEA
The lowest point that's not under water or ice is the shore of the Dead Sea. This salty inland sea borders Israel and Jordan. The shore is 1,312 feet (400 m) below **sea level**.

Challenger Deep Trench

CHALLENGER DEEP
Challenger Deep is the lowest point below sea level. This ocean trench is under the northwest Pacific Ocean. It is 35,840 feet (10,924 m) deep.

CHAPTER 2:
Earth's Layers

Earth's crust is the part of the planet we see and know best. Its tall mountains and deep valleys make the crust seem "rock solid." The bottom of the ocean seems a long way down. Yet, in reality, the crust is the thinnest of Earth's layers. If you think of Earth as an apple, the crust is only as thick as the apple's skin!

EARTH'S THIN CRUST

Earth's **landforms** are quite different from place to place. The thickness of the crust is also different. It is thicker where there are mountains and thinner in ocean trenches. On land, the crust is about 25 miles (40 km) at its thickest point. Beneath the oceans, the crust is generally just more than 4 miles (7 km) thick. Most of the planet is covered with water. About 70 percent of Earth's crust is under oceans.

Uluru is a rock formation in central Australia. Scientists believe it is the remains of an earlier mountain range. It is a good example of the amazing features on Earth's crust.

Viewing the Grand Canyon in Arizona enables you to see deep into Earth's surface. You can see the layers of the crust. The canyon is more than 1 mile (1.6 km) deep at its lowest point.

EARTH'S CRUST: THICK OR THIN?

Earth's crust is about 25 miles (40 km) thick where most people live. Try comparing that measurement to something you know.

1) At the start of your next trip, make a note of the mileage on the car. Note where you are after driving for 25 miles (40 km). Also note how long it took to get to that point. If it were possible to drive through the crust, that's how far you would have to travel!

2) Locate your hometown on a map. Then find another city or place you know that's about 25 miles (40 km) away.

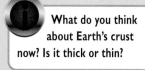 What do you think about Earth's crust now? Is it thick or thin?

THE MANTLE

The mantle is the layer beneath the crust. It is the thickest of Earth's layers. Its average depth is about 1,800 miles (2,900 km).

UPPER MANTLE

The upper part of the mantle is hard, like Earth's crust. Below that is a thinner layer called the **asthenosphere**. Things really start to heat up in this layer. Temperatures may reach 1,600° F (870° C). That's hot enough to melt some types of rocks! Scientists believe the asthenosphere is mostly solid. But under heat and pressure, it is soft enough to flow slowly. It may be more like honey or melted tar.

HOT SPOTS

A hot spot is an area of the upper mantle that is especially hot. Hot spots form when magma rises. It acts like a blowtorch that heats the crust. The country of Iceland is over a hot spot. People in Iceland can swim outdoors even in winter! Boiling magma comes close to the surface. It heats lakes and pools naturally.

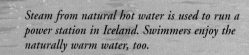

Steam from natural hot water is used to run a power station in Iceland. Swimmers enjoy the naturally warm water, too.

EARTH'S LAYERS

Earth's layers get hotter and hotter from the surface to the center. This diagram shows the thickness of each layer.

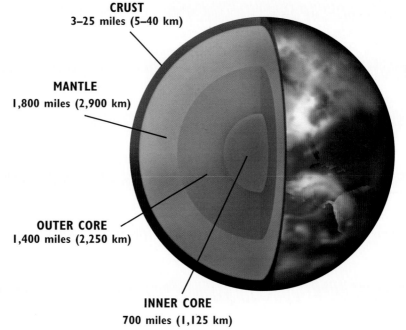

CRUST
3–25 miles (5–40 km)

MANTLE
1,800 miles (2,900 km)

OUTER CORE
1,400 miles (2,250 km)

INNER CORE
700 miles (1,125 km)

LOWER MANTLE

The rocks in the lower mantle are mostly made of oxygen, metals, and a mineral called silicon. Pressure and heat increase greatly in the lower mantle. Temperatures may reach nearly 4,000° F (2,200° C) at its deepest part.

Old Faithful shoots thousands of gallons of boiling water into the air every 76 minutes. It is part of the system of hot springs and pools at Yellowstone National Park, in Wyoming. The system may be fed by a hot spot.

JOURNEY TO THE CENTER OF THE EARTH

Scientists believe the average temperature in Earth's outer core is about 4,000° F (2,200° C).

In the inner core, temperatures are greater than 9,000° F (5,000° C). That is almost as hot as the surface of the Sun.

THE EARTH'S CORE

The core is the layer of Earth that scientists know the least about. They believe the core has two layers. The outer layer is hot and fluid. The inside layer is solid.

The outer core is made mainly of molten iron and nickel. It is almost 1,400 miles (2,250 km) thick.

The inner core is probably made of metals such as iron and nickel, too. The materials are under great pressure, so the core stays solid.

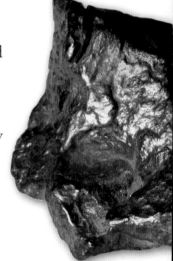

A blacksmith heats metal to make a horseshoe. The red-hot metal is softer than normal. It acts like the metals in Earth's outer core.

LIKE A BIG MAGNET

Earth's outer core is melted metal. This mass of metal moves. As it moves, it causes the solid inner core to spin. Scientists believe this motion, along with heat, creates a **magnetic field**. Earth behaves like a giant magnet.

Like a bar magnet, Earth has south and north magnetic poles. Earth's magnetic field makes a compass needle point north.

This meteorite was found in Arizona. The meteorite is made of iron and nickel. Those are the ingredients of Earth's core.

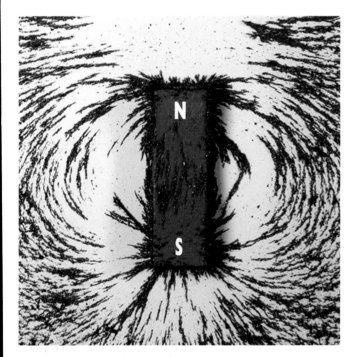

Earth acts like a giant bar magnet. Both have north and south poles. In this photo, small pieces of iron show the magnetic field around the magnet. If we could see Earth's magnetic field, it would look similar.

USE A COMPASS TO FIND YOUR WAY

The compass has been around a long time. Sailors and other travelers use compasses to point them in the right direction. But anyone can use a compass to find his or her way. Follow these steps to use a compass to create a closed shape. Then test your friends.

Materials needed
- a compass
- a tape measure
- paper
- a pen or pencil

1) Stand with the compass in your hand. Hold it as level as you can. The compass points north. Turn your body so you are facing east.

2) Use the chart below. Walk the different distances in the directions listed. Draw a picture of your path as you walk.
- Walk 30 feet (9 m) east.
- Walk 15 feet (4.5 m) southeast.
- Walk 15 feet (4.5 m) southwest.
- Walk 30 feet (9 m) west.
- Walk 15 feet (4.5 m) northwest.
- Walk 15 feet (4.5 m) northeast.

3) You should arrive at the point where you started. Look at the picture you drew of your path. What shape does it make?

4) On a separate sheet of paper, write down the directions listed above. Give them to a friend. Ask him or her to use a compass to follow the path and make a drawing along the way. Compare your picture with your friend's. Do they look alike?

CHAPTER 3:
Our Restless Earth

Look at the continents on a map of the world. Is it possible that if the landmasses were pushed together, they might fit like the pieces of a jigsaw puzzle? For example, would western Africa fit around eastern South America?

PANGAEA

In the early 1900s, German scientist Alfred Wegener (1880–1930) stated that Earth's continents were once one huge piece of land. He named the giant landmass **Pangaea**. The name means "all lands."

EARTH'S JIGSAW PUZZLE

Scientist believe that Earth's surface looked like this about 225 million years ago. A lot has changed over the last couple of hundred million years! Today, India is a part of Asia. Central America connects North America and South America. Long ago, India was an island. Central America had not even formed yet. Today, a person in the United States would need to take a plane or a boat to get to Africa. If people had been around back then, they could have made the trip on foot!

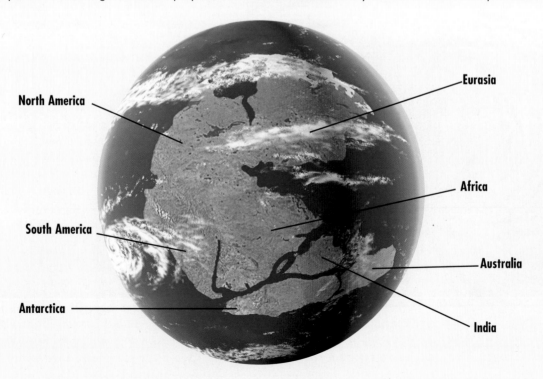

CONTINENTAL DRIFT

Over millions of years, Pangaea split apart. Separate landmasses formed. These landmasses became the continents we know today. This idea is known as **continental drift**. Over millions of years, the continents drifted to their current spots. And they are still moving!

Scientists have gathered evidence, or proof, to support this **theory**. A theory is an idea that needs to be proved. Scientists have found traces of dead plants and animals that match those on separate landmasses. They have proof that **glaciers**, slow-moving masses of ice, were once in places where there is no ice today. They can show that continents seem to fit together.

FOLLOW THE FOSSILS

Fossils are traces of dead plants or animals. Fossils can be bones or teeth. They can also be marks made in soft rock by a creature's body. Fossils of a prehistoric reptile shown below have been found in both South America and Africa. This seems to be proof that the two continents were once connected. This reptile lived only in **freshwater**. It could not have swum through the ocean from one continent to the other.

This view of Earth was created from images taken from space. The continents are still drifting very slowly. The world map may look very different millions of years from now!

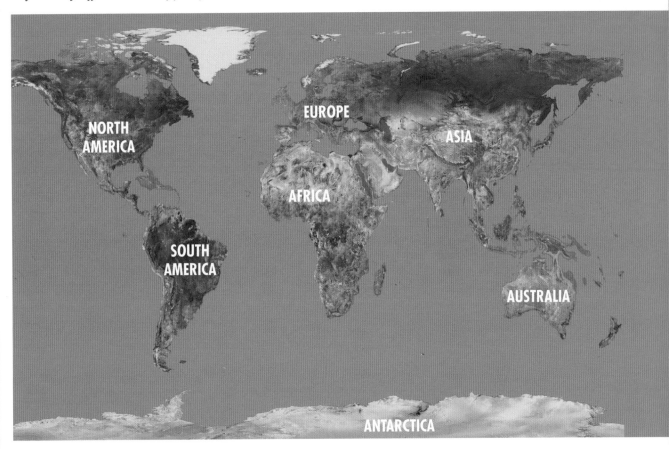

NORTH AMERICA

EUROPE

ASIA

AFRICA

SOUTH AMERICA

AUSTRALIA

ANTARCTICA

THE EARTH'S PLATES

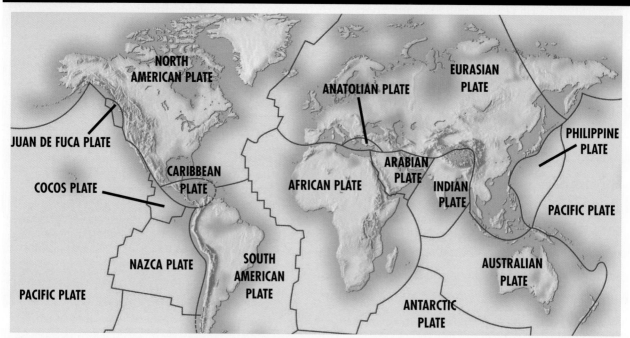

The continents are still moving. North America and Europe are slowly drifting apart. The Atlantic and Indian oceans get wider by a few centimeters each year. The Pacific Ocean is very slowly shrinking.

CITIES ON THE MOVE

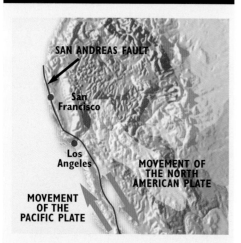

This map shows part of the West Coast of the Unites States. Two tectonic plates meet along the red line. That line shows the San Andreas Fault. The two plates are moving past each other. They move about 2 inches (5 centimeters) each year.

Think of where those plates might be in 15 million years. San Francisco and Los Angeles might be next to each other!

PLATE TECTONICS

Scientists continued to study Earth's crust. This lead to new discoveries. Earth's crust and upper mantle are known as the **lithosphere**. Scientists now know that area is broken into huge pieces. The pieces are called **tectonic plates**.

These plates are big enough to support the continents and oceans. Yet they are always moving. They float on the liquid mantle below. The plates move just a few centimeters each year.

Scientists now know the movement of the plates causes much of the change in Earth's crust.

FAULTS

As tectonic plates move, they run over rocks underground. They press down on the rocks and stretch them. Huge pressure builds up. Sometimes there is so much pressure that cracks appear. The places where the crust cracks are called **faults**.

The San Andreas Fault runs along the Pacific coast of the United States. It is almost 800 miles (1,290 km) long.

EARTH'S CRACKED-UP CRUST

Materials needed

• a clear glass mixing bowl
• honey
• crackers

1) Pour the honey into the bowl. Make sure the bowl is about half full.

2) Carefully drop a few crackers onto the honey.

3) Imagine that the honey is Earth's liquid mantle. The crackers are the tectonic plates. What do you observe?

> Earth's mantle is molten, but it is also thick. The mantle material is thick enough to support the crust, just as the thick honey supports the crackers.

4) Now push one cracker with your finger. How easily does it move across the honey? What happens when one cracker moves against another?

> Crackers in the bowl will not have much room to move. When you move one cracker, those next to it will also move. The same is true of Earth's plates.

INSIDE A VOLCANO

A volcano is an opening in Earth's crust. Magma travels from the mantle up through a central vent. The vent is like a chimney. Rocks, gases, and lava shoot or spill out of the top of the vent. After each eruption, lava hardens and builds up. This makes the sides of the volcano steeper.

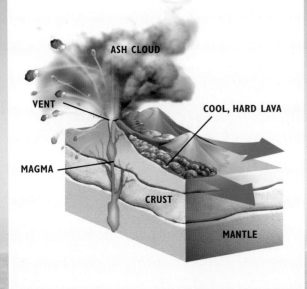

ASH CLOUD

VENT

COOL, HARD LAVA

MAGMA

CRUST

MANTLE

CHAPTER 4:
Changing Face of Earth

Many of the forces that created Earth still affect the planet today. Earthquakes and erupting volcanoes continue to shape the planet's surface. They are signs of activity within the planet's crust, mantle, and core.

VOLCANOES

Earth is dotted with volcanoes. Some are on the land. Some lie under the oceans. Many of Earth's volcanoes are along the edges of the tectonic plates.

EARTH'S RING OF FIRE

An active volcano is one that has erupted in recorded history. Earth has more than 500 active volcanoes. This total does not include the large number of volcanoes in the oceans. Many volcanoes are located along the Ring of Fire. That is a very active line of volcanoes around the Pacific Ocean. That area also has a lot of earthquakes.

ASIA

NORTH AMERICA

PACIFIC OCEAN

SOUTH AMERICA

AUSTRALIA

THE RING OF FIRE IS SHOWN IN ORANGE.

Some volcanoes erupt along the ocean ridges. That happens as plates move apart. Others form where an ocean plate meets a continental plate. Yet others rise up in the middle of a plate. Those kinds of volcanoes are created by hot spots.

Volcanoes are of special interest to scientists. The lava gives scientists a look at matter from inside our planet. It also gives them clues about activity below Earth's crust.

Sometimes magma breaks through Earth's crust at a hot spot. When this happens under the ocean, islands can form. Every time a volcano erupts, it grows bigger. As the lava builds up, it can break through the ocean's surface. It can form a volcanic island. The Hawaiian Islands were formed this way.

IDENTIFYING LAVA

Lava takes different forms. It can be smooth or crumbly. It can form big blocky chunks. The form lava takes depends on:

- what it is made of
- how much gas is in it
- the temperature of the flow

PAHOEHOE (pah-HOH-ee-hoh-ee) FLOW
This type of lava moves fast and looks as though it has wrinkles!

AA (AH-ah) FLOW
This type of lava moves slowly. It is coarse and may be sticky.

PILLOW FLOW
This type of lava is found underwater.

FAULT LINES

During an earthquake, the crust can break along a fault. The rock on either side of the fault shifts. It moves sideways or up or down.

NORMAL FAULT
At a normal fault, plates move away from each other.

REVERSE FAULT (DIP-SLIP)
Plates move toward each other at a reverse, or dip-slip, fault.

SLIP FAULT (STRIKE-SLIP)
At a slip fault, plates move past each other in a side-by-side path.

EARTHQUAKES

An earthquake is a sudden movement in Earth's crust that results from a buildup of pressure inside Earth. An earthquake begins as pressure builds along a fault. The two sides of a fault try to slip past each other. But they get stuck. The pressure builds underground. The crust bends. Sometimes the bending does not stop the pressure. Suddenly, rocks break and give way miles underground. Movement called **seismic waves** are sent out. They make the ground on the surface shake—an earthquake!

SEISMOGRAMS

A **seismograph** is a machine that traces the waves caused by an earthquake. The machine makes a paper record. This record, called a **seismogram**, shows the strength and duration of an earthquake.

TSUNAMIS

Earthquakes can happen at underwater faults, too. When they do, this can cause a **tsunami**—a giant wave. The waves ring out from the earthquake's **epicenter**. The epicenter is a spot below ground. It is the place just above where the earthquake starts.

The waves can move out across the ocean at hundreds of miles per hour. At the start, the waves may be small. But they change as they move toward land and shallow waters. There, they slow and start to build. As tsunami waves hit the shore, they can be nearly 100 feet (30 m) tall! A tsunami can be deadly.

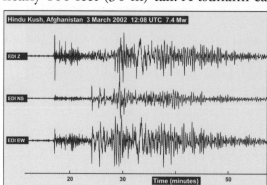

This is the seismogram of an earthquake in Afghanistan in 2002. The bigger the earthquake, the bigger the peaks that appear on the paper.

Workers search the rubble following an earthquake in Pisco, Peru. The August 2007 earthquake had a magnitude of 8.

MEASURING EARTHQUAKES

The strength of an earthquake is called its **magnitude**. The strength is measured by a scale called the **Moment Magnitude Scale**. An earthquake of the lowest magnitude is hard to measure. An earthquake with a high magnitude is deadly! The world's largest earthquake was recorded in Chile on May 22, 1960. Its magnitude was 9.5. Thousands of people were killed or injured. Another two million lost their homes.

MAGMA UNDER PRESSURE

Do you want to learn how magma is forced up to Earth's surface? Just grab a tube of toothpaste!

Materials needed
• a tube of toothpaste   • a toothpick or skewer

1) Make sure the top to the toothpaste tube is screwed on tightly.

2) Use your fingers to put pressure on the tube in different places. Observe how the toothpaste in the tube moves away from the pressure.

3) Now poke a small hole in the tube. Squeeze again. Toothpaste should start to ooze from the hole.

Magma is under great pressure inside Earth. Heat and weight press from above. The molten rock seeks the nearest open space. The tube of toothpaste is like a volcano that allows magma (the toothpaste) to escape the great pressure.

MAKING MOUNTAINS

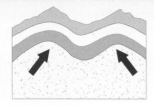

FOLD MOUNTAINS

The movements of the plates can force rocks to push against each other. They can fold down to make valleys or fold up to make mountains.

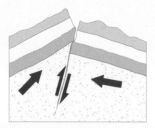

FAULT MOUNTAINS

Sometimes Earth's surface cracks on a fault. Layers of rock on one side can be pushed up to form a mountain.

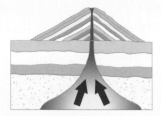

VOLCANIC MOUNTAINS

Some mountains are formed by volcanic activity. These mountains are formed from lava and rocks. After an eruption, lava hardens and cools on the surface.

DOME MOUNTAINS

Sometimes heat from inside the mantle pushes Earth's crust up. This creates a bulge on the surface.

AN EVER-CHANGING PICTURE

Earth's crust is always changing. Natural forces from below, such as heat, pressure, and movement, cause these changes. Weather causes changes on the surface. That is a long, slow process.

MOUNTAINS

Mountains are changing features on Earth. Mountains are formed when tectonic plates move. Sometimes the plates hit head on. Sometimes they move against each other. As they do, their edges are changed. This causes huge, rocky landforms to appear. On Earth's surface, mountains rise. It can take thousands or millions of years for a mountain to form.

WIND AND WATER

Earth's crust is also shaped by forces such as **weathering** and **erosion**. Weathering is the breakdown of rock. Over time, wind and water wear away rock. Its surface breaks apart. Then erosion takes over. Wind, water, and ice carry the sediment away. All kinds of interesting things form. The rock formation shown here is in Utah. It is called the Three Gossips. It shows the results of weathering and erosion over time.

The Andes Mountains in South America are the world's longest chain of mountains. They were formed about 70 million years ago, when the Nazca Plate hit the South American Plate.

WATER AT WORK

Water is another factor in the changes on Earth's surface. As a river runs its course, it cuts into land. A river can make a valley in Earth's crust. A river can also carry bits of sand and soil, called **sediment**, from one place to another. The ocean changes landmasses, too. It crashes into the shore, creating cliffs.

The Andes Mountains stretch along the west coast of South America. They are an example of fold mountains. The Andes chain has many volcanic mountains.

The Gorges du Verdon is in France. This valley is being formed as the Verdon River cuts its path. Notice the V shape of the valley. A V-shaped valley is a sign of a young stream.

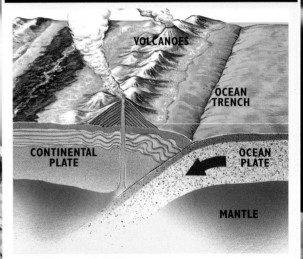

IN THE TRENCHES

Sometimes one tectonic plate forces another plate to fall below it. This is called **subduction**. In the ocean, this activity can result in deep trenches.

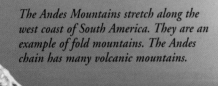

Marble is a metamorphic rock. It is formed when limestone comes under great heat and pressure. For centuries, marble has been used for statues. Today, your kitchen surfaces might be marble.

These sandstone forms are in Antelope Canyon in Arizona. They were made by powerful, rushing floodwaters.

CHAPTER 5:
Earth's Building Blocks

The crust of our planet is made of rock. The tectonic plates move rock. They crunch and fold it. They force rock up from deep underground. Volcanoes heat underground rocks. The hot rocks rise to the surface. Rocks are always on the move and changing.

ROCK FEST

The rocks of Earth's crust are made mainly from eight elements. The way these elements combine creates different kinds of rock. Scientists separate Earth's rocks into three main groups.

Igneous rocks are formed from molten magma that has cooled and become solid.

SOIL: THE BASIS FOR LIFE

Soil is everywhere. It's easy to forget how important it is. Without soil, plants couldn't grow. Plants produce the oxygen that humans and animals breathe. So we need soil to survive. This chart shows what makes up soil.

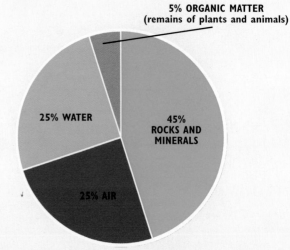

5% ORGANIC MATTER
(remains of plants and animals)

25% WATER

45% ROCKS AND MINERALS

25% AIR

Soil is created by weathering. Grains of rock and minerals mix with air, water, and other materials. Soil differs from place to place. Its basic ingredients, however, remain the same.

THE ROCK CYCLE

**The rock cycle changes rocks from one type into another.
This process is happening around us and under our feet all the time!**

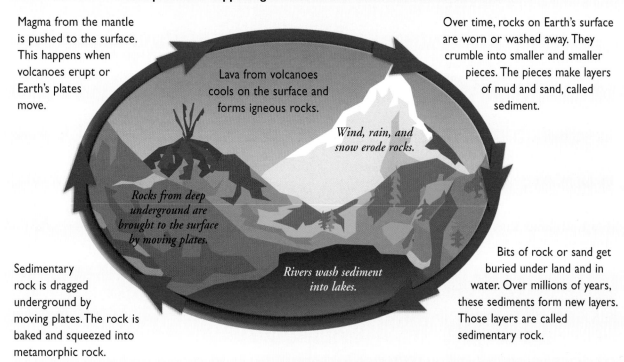

Magma from the mantle is pushed to the surface. This happens when volcanoes erupt or Earth's plates move.

Lava from volcanoes cools on the surface and forms igneous rocks.

Over time, rocks on Earth's surface are worn or washed away. They crumble into smaller and smaller pieces. The pieces make layers of mud and sand, called sediment.

Wind, rain, and snow erode rocks.

Rocks from deep underground are brought to the surface by moving plates.

Sedimentary rock is dragged underground by moving plates. The rock is baked and squeezed into metamorphic rock.

Rivers wash sediment into lakes.

Bits of rock or sand get buried under land and in water. Over millions of years, these sediments form new layers. Those layers are called sedimentary rock.

Sedimentary rocks are formed from sediment, or tiny grains of sand and soil. Sedimentary rocks form on land or in water. They form wherever sediment is left behind. Over many years, sediments join together and form rocks.

Metamorphic rocks are rocks that have changed from either igneous or sedimentary rocks. Heat and pressure deep within Earth changed them into a new form of rock.

This mountain shows signs of exfoliation. That is when sheets of rock break off. The rock is then broken up into sediment. Waterfalls and streams in the mountains carry the sediment away.

SCIENTISTS IN ACTION

Figuring out Earth's mysteries takes many kinds of scientists. Those who study Earth include:

GEOLOGISTS
Geologists study Earth's structure, including rocks and rock formations.

HYDROGEOLOGISTS
Hydrogeologists study how water moves through Earth's soil and rocks.

MINERALOGISTS
These professional "rock collectors" study rocks, gemstones, and other minerals.

SEISMOLOGISTS
Seismologists study earthquakes and seismic waves.

VOLCANOLOGISTS
Volcanologists study old volcanic deposits and new eruptions. With modern equipment, volcanologists can predict future eruptions. This can help to save thousands of lives!

STILL SEARCHING FOR ANSWERS

Every day, it seems, we improve our ability to investigate our world. After an earthquake, scientists worldwide can find information about it on the Internet. They can look up the epicenter. They can see the magnitude of the quake. They can study the length and depth of the fault line.

Sharing core and crust information is important. A recent project in California is a good example. Scientists placed 250 global positioning system (GPS) instruments along the San Andreas Fault. These instruments record changes in the crust. This project will be part of a bigger project. It is being run by a group known as EarthScope. These scientists will watch the entire North American continent.

SCIENTIFIC FORECASTING

Scientists want to be able to forecast earthquakes. They want to know when volcanoes will erupt. Knowing when these events will happen would help save lives.

KNOWING IF AND WHEN

Who or what might be in the path of lava? How much time do people need to get out of the way? With the help of computers, scientists can study a volcano's activity. They can study its eruptions, the changes in its shape, and more. This information can help scientists forecast the next event. The International Volcano Research Center, in Arizona, has created such a program. It has been in use since 1988. The center has been right in more than 90 percent of its forecasts.

Learning about Earth and how it acts is important. Earth science is a matter of building upon ideas—yours, a fellow scientist's, history's. Who knows where the next "big idea" will arise?

A team of geologists reached this summit crater in December 2005. They are atop Mount Erebus. It is the most active volcano in Antarctica. A lake of lava sits at the bottom of the crater.

SEEING EARTH AS A SYSTEM

Events on Earth affect life all over the planet. An earthquake causes a tsunami that crushes a coastline. A plate of land hits another and folds into a mountain. A volcano erupts and covers a town in ash.

Scientists see Earth as one system. They see everything that happens as connected. NASA is the U.S. space agency. As part of its Earth Science program, scientists study the land, water, and air.

The program has three parts:
1) satellites to watch the planet and collect information
2) a system to review the information
3) a team of scientists to study the information

SG-3

Geologists from many countries have used deep drilling to learn more about Earth's crust. On May 24, 1970, a team from the former Soviet Union began drilling in the Kola Peninsula in the Arctic. They drilled for 24 years, digging a hole more than 7 miles (11 km) deep. The Soviets did not get through the crust. But they did discover rocks that had not been seen before. Geologists had theories of what rocks at that depth would be like. Now they can compare the real rocks with their theories. The hole, called SG-3, is still the deepest hole made by humans.

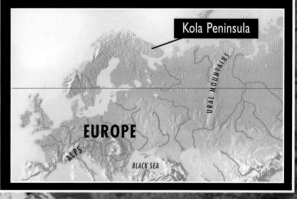

Kola Peninsula

URAL MOUNTAINS

EUROPE

ALPS

BLACK SEA

GLOSSARY

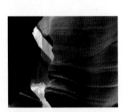

asteroid: a space rock, bigger than a meteor, that orbits the Sun

asthenosphere: the thin layer of Earth's upper mantle. It is somewhat liquid, so the solid crust moves on it.

atmosphere: the thick layer of air that surrounds the Earth. The gases that make up Earth's atmosphere include nitrogen (78 percent) and oxygen (21 percent).

comet: a ball of frozen gas, dust, and rock

continental drift: a theory that all the continents once formed a giant landmass but moved apart over millions of years

core: the center of Earth. The core is made up of an inner core and an outer core. Earth's core is about 2,100 miles (3,375 km) thick.

crust: the outer layer of Earth that consists of landforms and the ocean floor. The crust is about 25 miles (40 km) at its thickest point.

diameter: the distance measured by a straight line through the center of a circle or sphere, reaching from side to side

earthquake: a fierce shaking of the ground caused by rocks cracking and breaking deep underground

element: a substance made up of a single type of atom. Elements can't be broken into simpler components by chemical processes.

epicenter: the point on the surface that is directly above where an earthquake began

erosion: the wearing away of material by water, wind, or glacial ice

fault: a crack in Earth's crust where huge blocks of rock slide past each other

fossil: the remains or traces of a living thing that died long ago

freshwater: water that is not salty and that can be used by humans, animals, and plants. The water in ponds, lakes, rivers, and streams is usually freshwater.

glacier: a large body of ice that moves slowly down a slope or valley or spreads out on the surface of the land

igneous rock: rocks formed from magma that has reached Earth's surface and cooled

impact crater: a hole on Earth's surface that is caused by an object from space

landform: a feature on Earth's surface, such as a mountain

lava: molten matter from a volcano or a break in Earth's surface. Before it reaches the surface, this matter is known as magma.

lithosphere: the hard outer layer of Earth. The lithosphere is formed from the crust and the uppermost part of the mantle.

magma: molten rock in Earth's mantle and outer core. Magma that reaches the surface is called lava.

magnetic field: the area around a magnet where the force of magnetism can be felt

magnitude: a measurement of the energy released during an earthquake

mantle: the thick layer of Earth that lies between the crust and core. The mantle is about 1,800 miles (2,900 km) thick.

matter: anything that has weight and takes up space. The three states of matter are solid, liquid, and gas.

metamorphic rock: a rock that forms when heat or pressure changes an igneous or a sedimentary rock

meteor: a chunk of rock and metal. A meteor that hits Earth is called a meteorite.

Moment Magnitude Scale: the scale used by scientists to measure the strength and size of an earthquake

orbit: to move in a circle around another object, such the planets circle the Sun

Pangaea: the name of the large landmass thought to exist about 250 million years ago. Pangaea was made up of all the landmasses that form today's continents.

radius: the length of a line from the edge of a circle or sphere to its center, or from the center to the edge

satellite: a body that revolves around another larger body in space. The Moon is Earth's only natural satellite.

sea level: the level of the sea's surface. Sea level is used for measuring the height or depth of land and landforms.

sediment: sand and soil carried by water, wind, or glaciers

sedimentary rock: rock formed from bits of soil and sand called sediment. Over time, the sediment is crushed into layers and forms new rock.

seismic waves: energy that ripples out from an earthquake

seismogram: a printed record of the information recorded by a seismograph

seismograph: an instrument that detects, measures, and records vibrations in Earth at a specific location

solar system: a group of planets orbiting a star, such as our Sun

subduction: the process in which part of a tectonic plate moves beneath another

tectonic plate: a giant piece of Earth's crust that floats on Earth's mantle. Plates are always moving at a very slow rate.

theory: an idea that explains how or why something happens

tsunami: a huge and harmful ocean wave caused by an earthquake under the ocean

volcano: a hole in Earth's crust through which gas, ash, and magma escape

water vapor: a gas that is produced when water evaporates

weathering: the breakdown of rock over a long period of time by factors such as wind and water

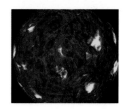